AF480534

Shapes That Race

Written **and** Illustrated
by **Stephanie Francis**

This book
belongs to:

____

Circle lived in the land of shapes.

He had four best friends,
Square,
Triangle,
Rectangle,
and Diamond.

Circle was the friendliest of all the shapes.
Whenever he walked down the street, he smiled and waved.

Everybody loved Circle except for Oval.
Oval was upset and did not like Circle because he had a new toy car

8

Oval went over to Circle
and said,
Do you want to run
a race with me?

What are we racing for?
Circle said.
Let's race for our toys
to see who is the fastest runner
said Oval.

10

If you win, you can play
with my baseball.
If I win, I can play
with your new toy car.

Okay! Circle said.
Let's meet today at 1:30 pm
at the race park. Oval replied.

Circle was so excited, that he ran down the street to tell all of his friends about the race.

Good luck guys! Diamond said.
Both runners were sure
they could win the race.

Triangle yelled!
On your mark, get set, Go!
Oval had a great start
and was in the lead.

But Circle passed him by quickly.

Go, Go, Go!
His friends cheered him on.

He ran as fast as he could
to the finish line
and won the race.

Oval was very upset
that he had lost the race.

A deal is a deal!

He said as he
handed Circle his baseball.
Even though Oval lost the race,
Circle still lent him his new toy car.

20

Now all the shapes can
play a baseball game together.

The End.

Race

With Shapes
And Learn
Their Names.

Circle

Triangle

Square

Oval

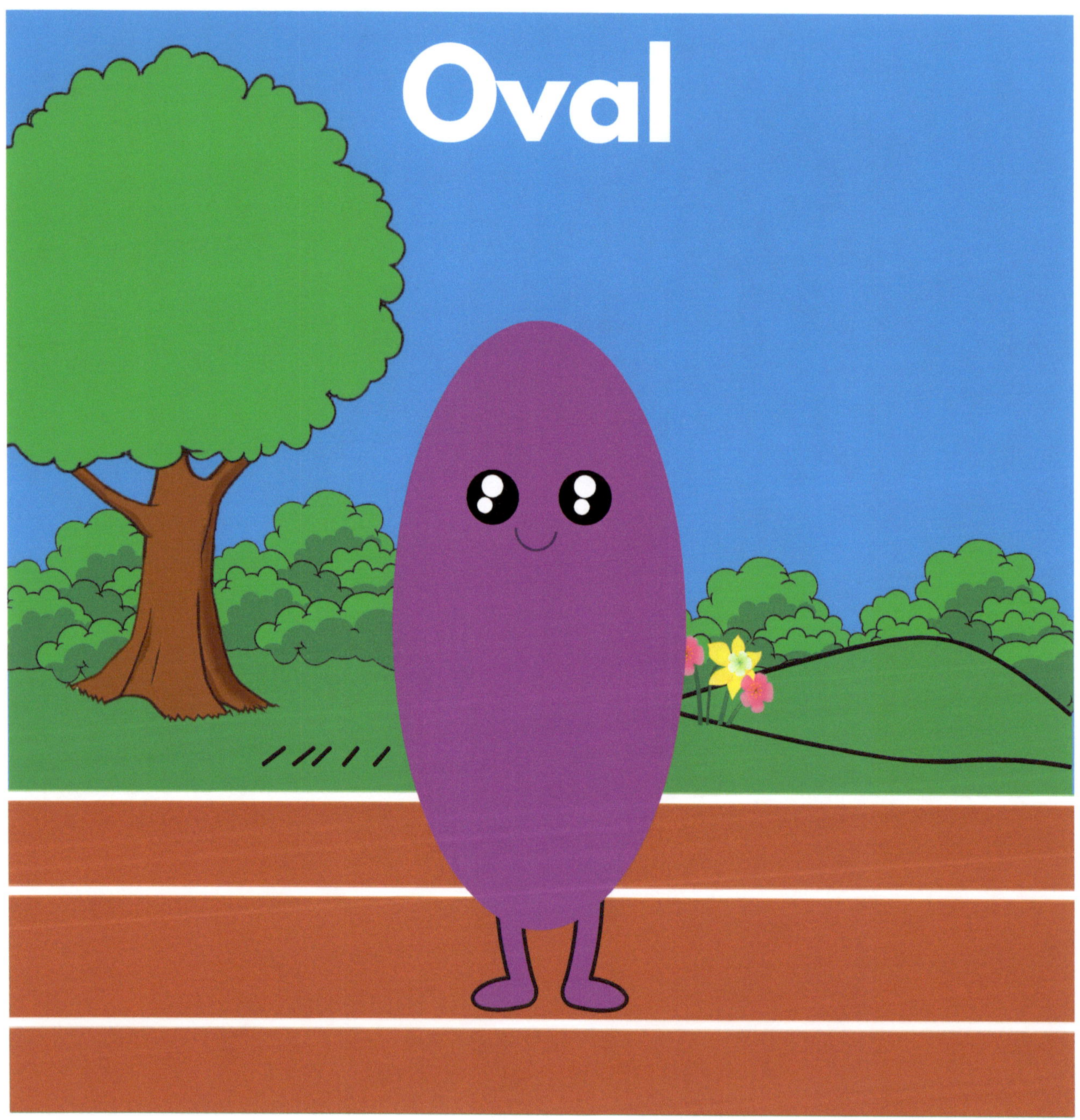

Octagon

Diamond
(Rhombus)

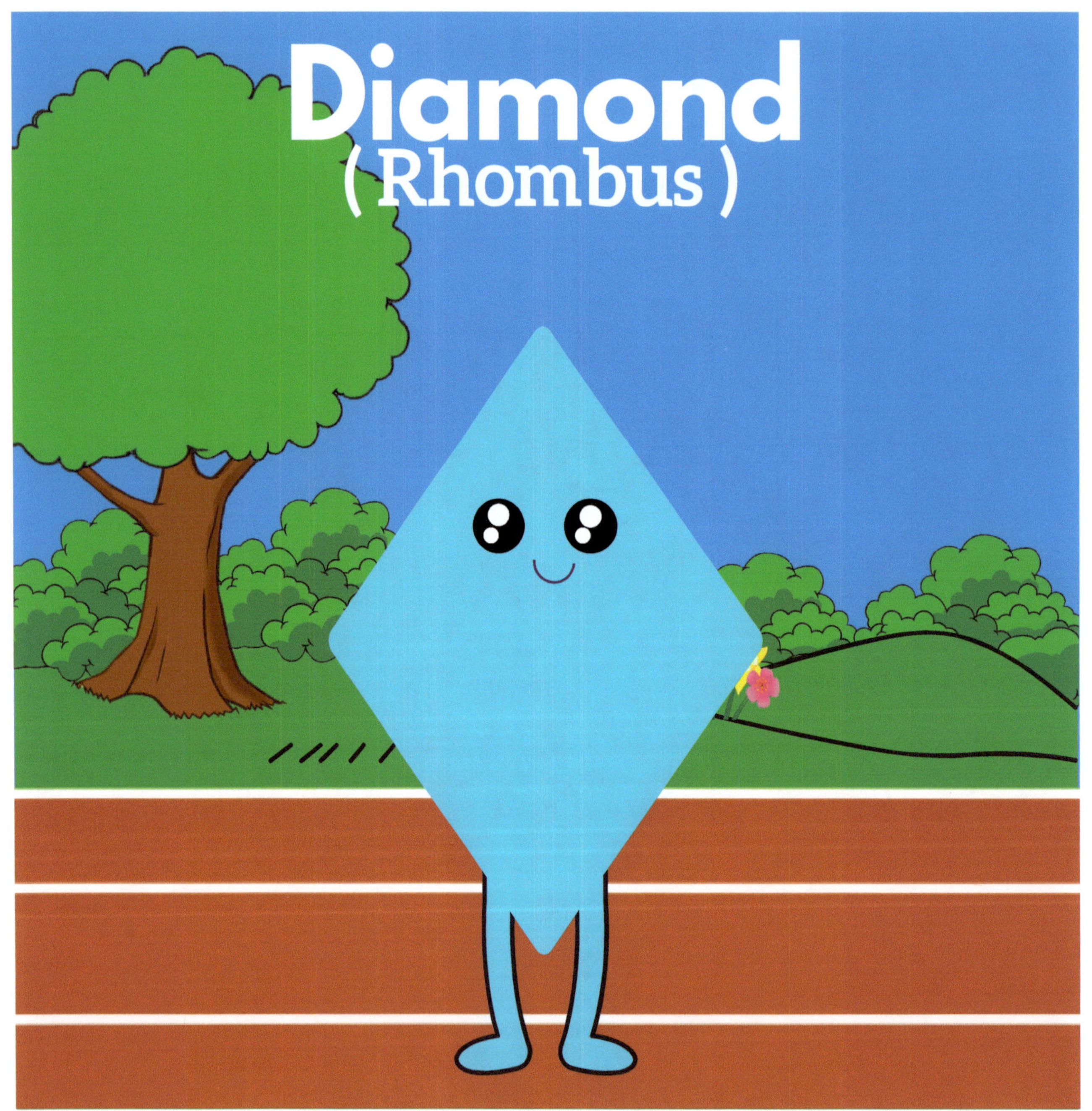

Cross

Trapezoid

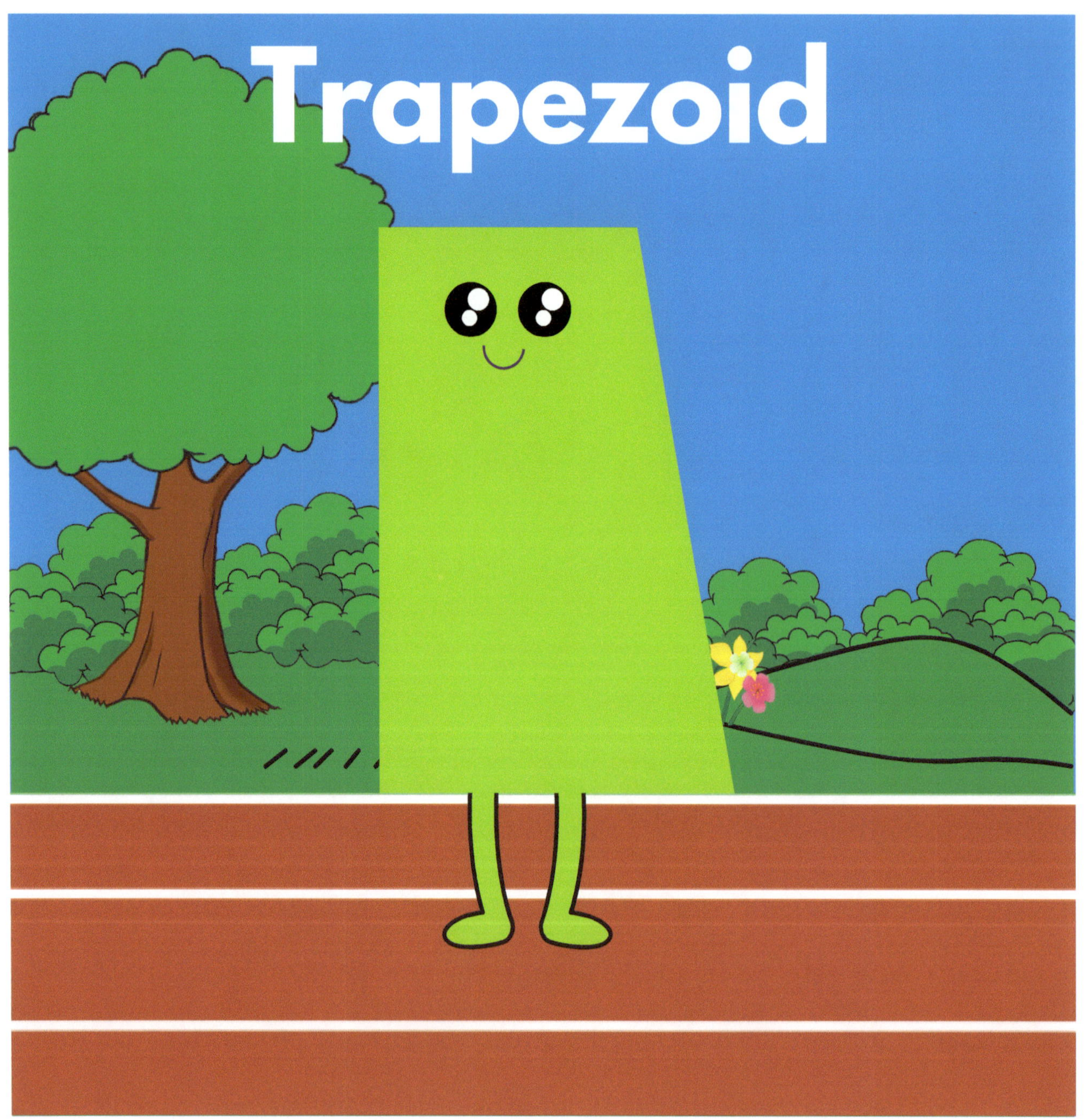

Arrow

Star

Heart

Parallelogram

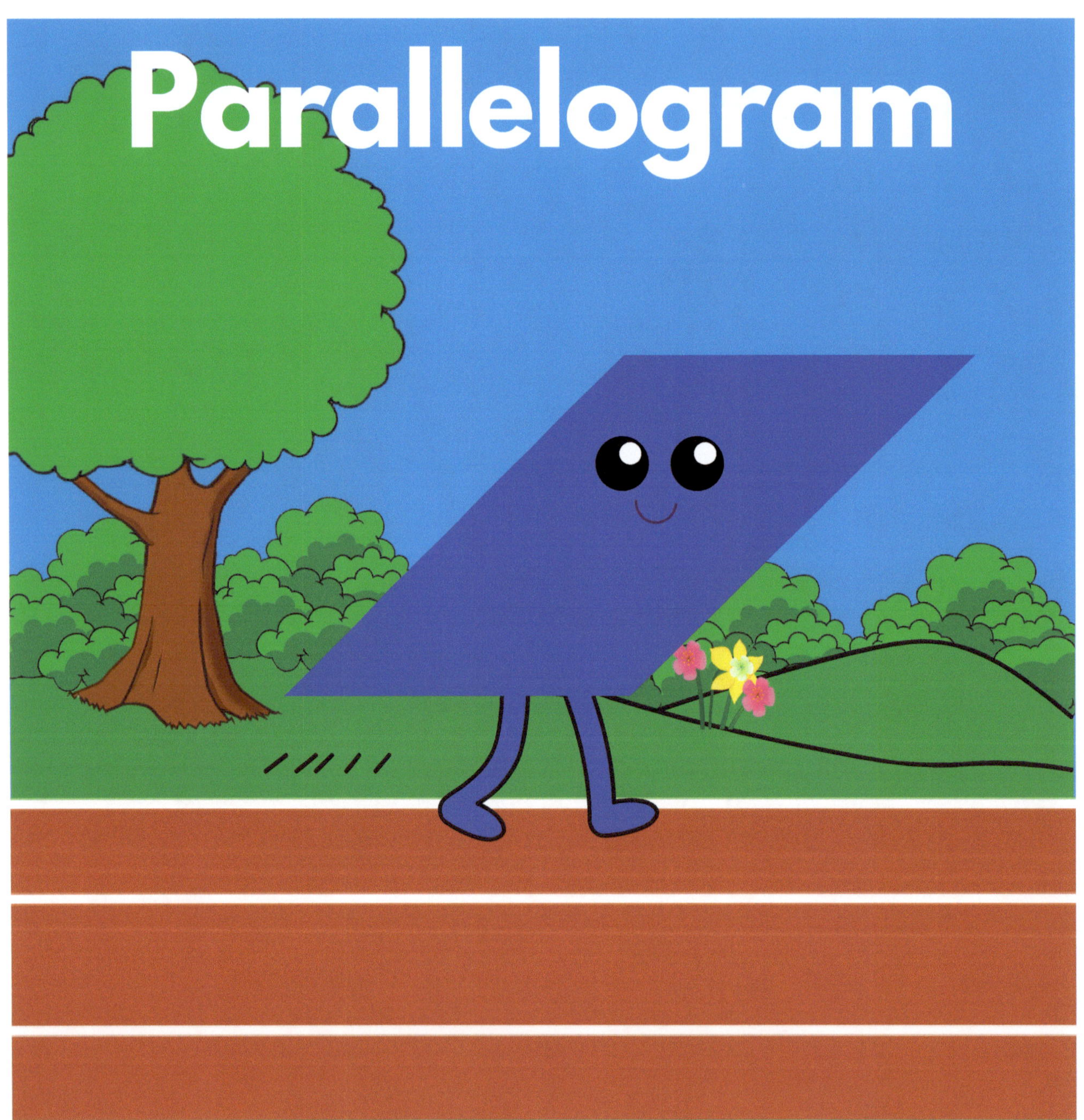

Crescent

Rectangle

Pentagon

Hexagon

Semicircle

Index

www.ingramcontent.com/pod-product-compliance
Lightning Source LLC
Chambersburg PA
CBHW042057110726
48006CB00002B/433